The Slumber Party

story by Margaret Wild ★ pictures by David Cox

TICKNOR & FIELDS

Books for Young Readers

New York · 1993

93331

First American edition 1993 published by Ticknor & Fields,
A Houghton Mifflin company,
215 Park Avenue South, New York, New York 10003.

First published in Australia by Omnibus Books

Manufactured in the United States of America.

Text of this book is set in 16pt. ITC Clearface Regular.
The illustrations are watercolor, reproduced in full color.

HOR 10 9 8 7 6 5 4 3 2 1

Library of Congress Cataloging-in-Publication Data

Wild, Margaret.
    The slumber party / written by Margaret Wild ; illustrated by
David Cox. — 1st American ed.
        p.   cm.
    Summary: Jane's birthday sleepover is a night of games, a lost
mouse, a croaking frog, a little sleep, and a lot of fun.
    ISBN 0-395-66598-1
    [1. Sleepovers—Fiction.   2. Birthdays—Fiction.]
I. Cox, David,   ill.   II. Title.
PZ7.W64574Sl   1993
[E]—dc20   92-39783   CIP   AC

This one's for Karen

—M.W.

JANE invites seven friends to her birthday slumber party:
Kusum, Pete, Kathy, Liam, Mei-Lin, Cassie, and Emma.
Jane's big brother, Tom, is glad their cousin Brenda is
also coming. He and Brenda have plans...

Getting Ready

Mei-Lin packs her toy frog, her frog pin, and her frog slippers. Then she puts her pet frog, Cannibal, down the front of her sweater. She does not want to leave him at home.

Liam packs his summer space suit pajamas. His mother says he will get cold at night, but he won't listen.

Emma packs her favorite barrettes and headbands for her best friend, Kusum. Kusum likes doing things with her hair.

Kusum packs her shampoo,
her red hairbrush and comb,
and her red headband.

No one remembers to pack a
toothbrush, except Cassie.
She has an electric toothbrush.
She brushes her teeth all the time.

Kathy packs her warm pajamas, her robe, her slippers, clothes for the next day, her raincoat, her rubber boots, her flashlight, and her first-aid kit. Kathy likes to be well-prepared.

Brenda packs her water gun, some water balloons, her plastic doggie doo, and her black rubber spider.

Pete can't find his fuzzy yellow monkey anywhere. His baby sister, Jo, says he can have one of her pacifiers instead. She has a suitcase full of pacifiers.

Pete says, "I'm not a baby like you! Go away!"
He crawls under the bed and says he won't go
to the party without his yellow monkey.

Jo goes looking...

At the Party

Jane opens all her presents.
She shows everyone her favorite
gift from her family: a little
white mouse named Curly.
Everyone wants to pet him.

Curly runs down Brenda's leg
and disappears behind the furniture.

Jane cries, and her mother says, "Don't worry, dear. He's sure to turn up." They put breadcrumbs and pieces of cheese all over the house, but Curly won't come out.

They all play Simon Says, and Mei-Lin wins. Tom sulks. He likes to win.

Emma tries to eat her lasagne, but she's not hungry. Her best friend, Kusum, is sitting next to Kathy. Every now and then they look at Emma and laugh. Emma wishes she were back home.

Brenda sneaks her black rubber spider onto Liam's plate. He says, "I know it's fake, silly."

He throws it at Brenda, but it lands on the cake.

Tom licks off the icing and pretends to bite off the spider's legs. He says, "I just love eating squishy-squashy spiders. Their insides are all green!"

"You're disgusting!" Jane shouts.
She throws purple cupcakes at Tom.

Cassie plugs in her electric toothbrush. She uses pink icing instead of toothpaste. Brenda and Tom decide they like Cassie. They want to sit next to her while they watch a movie.

During the scary part, Cannibal leaps out of Mei-Lin's sweater and hops on Jane's father. He says he has a headache.

Pete sits on the plastic doggie doo. He yells. Tom and Brenda fall down laughing.

Bedtime

Mei-Lin and Cannibal snuggle up in the sleeping-bag. Every now and again Cannibal gives a contented croak.

Jane can't fall asleep. She's worried about Curly. She hopes the cat next door won't get him.

Tom and Cassie have a pillow fight.

Kathy and Brenda have a pillow fight.
Soon everyone is in the pillow fight.

THAT'S ENOUGH, BED NOW!

Emma feels sad because her best friend, Kusum, is sleeping next to Kathy. They are telling secrets.

Emma cries, but no one hears her.

Cassie brushes her teeth again. None of the others remember to brush their teeth.

Brenda drops a water balloon on Tom.

Tom squirts Brenda with the water gun.

Liam is freezing in his summer space suit pajamas. He wishes he had his green sweatsuit. He puts on his sweater and dirty socks, but he shivers all night.

Tom, Brenda, and Cassie slide down the banisters, and then go *thump thump* up the stairs.

Brenda and Tom sneak out to the kitchen
to have a midnight feast. They eat the rest
of the birthday cake. Tom feels sick, but
Brenda eats half a jar of dill pickles and
the next day's chicken.

At two o'clock in the morning the little white mouse peeps out from behind the refrigerator. He nibbles at some cheese.

Then he scampers up the stairs

—and into Jane's mom and dad's bed.

Jane's mom and dad jump out of bed—fast!
They switch on the light and throw back the covers.
Curly blinks up at them. He's sleepy and warm.

Just before dawn Pete wakes up. For a moment he doesn't know where he is. Then he remembers, and hugs his yellow monkey. He's glad Jo found it for him. He has saved a slice of birthday cake wrapped up in a napkin to take home for Jo.

Going Home

Jane says it was the best
birthday party she ever had.
She can't stop petting Curly.
She's glad her dad's big
bottom didn't squash him.

After Jane's dad has made everyone breakfast, he goes back to bed. He still has a headache. He looks under the covers twice before climbing in.

Cassie brushes her teeth. Six times.

Jane's mom says, "How come there's no toothpaste left?"

Brenda looks everywhere for her plastic doggie doo.

Pete doesn't say anything, but he breaks into a little smile.

Kusum tells Emma she's sorry she was so mean. She says Emma is her best best friend. Kusum and Emma do each other's hair.

Kathy takes forever to pack her bag.
She's got too much stuff. Next time she'll
leave her flashlight at home. She pretends not
to notice Kusum and Emma together.

Liam tells his mother that
of course he wasn't cold.
He's happy he wore his
summer space suit pajamas.
So there!

Mei-Lin takes Cannibal upstairs to say good-bye to Jane's dad.

He puts a pillow over his head. He doesn't want to kiss Cannibal good-bye.

Tom asks Cassie to come and play the next day. He says she can borrow his skateboard, if he can use her electric toothbrush. Cassie says, "Okay." She likes Tom.

At home, Pete gives Jo the slice of birthday cake. Jo loves Pete. She wants to give him something, too.

She empties her suitcase of chewed up, soggy pacifiers into Pete's bed. He will have a nice surprise tonight.

Pete starts planning his birthday slumber party. So do Kusum, Liam, Cassie, Kathy, Mei-Lin, Emma, and Tom. Brenda cackles to herself. She's going to have a vampire slumber party—just wait and see!